If You'll Be My Valentine

BY CYNTHIA RYLANT

ILLUSTRATED BY FUMI KOSAKA

HarperCollins*Publishers*

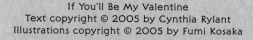

Library of Congress Cataloging-in-Publication Data
Rylant, Cynthia. • If you'll be my Valentine / by Cynthia Rylant ;
illustrated by Fumi Kosaka.—1st ed. • p. cm. • Summary: A little boy gives
Valentines out to friends and family. •
ISBN-10: 0-06-009270-X (trade bdg.) — ISBN-13: 978-0-06-009270-2 (trade bdg.) •
ISBN-10: 0-06-009269-6 (lib. bdg.) — ISBN-13: 978-0-06-009269-6 (lib. bdg.) •
ISBN-10: 0-06-009271-8 (pbk.) — ISBN-13: 978-0-06-009271-9 (pbk.) •
[1. Valentines—Fiction. 2. Valentine's Day—Fiction. 3. Stories in rhyme.]
I. Title: If you will be my Valentine. II. Kosaka, Fumi, ill. III.
Title. • PZ8.3.R96If 2005 [E]—dc22 • 2003024271
Typography by Stephanie Bart-Horvath
❖
09 10 11 12 13 SCP 10 9 8 7 6 5

For Boris and Blossom, my furry friends
—C.R.

For my valentine, Tim
—F.K.

If you'll be my valentine
I'll kiss you on the nose.
I'll scratch your ears
and rub your head
and pet your little toes.

If you'll be my valentine
I'll give you extra treaties.
I'll give you two
and maybe three
and let you lick my feeties.

If you'll be my valentine
I'll take you on a walk.
I'll pull the wagon
just for you
and we can sing and talk.

If you'll be my valentine
I'll write a special letter.
I'll add some hugs
and kisses, too,
to make it even better.

If you'll be my valentine
I'll sit with you today.
We'll read a book
about some frogs
if you don't want to play.

If you'll be my valentine
I'll take you in my car.
You'll sit up front
so you can look.
But we won't go too far.

If you'll be my valentine
I'll sing a song for you.
And when you fly
up in the sky
then you can sing one, too.

If you'll be my valentine
I'll pour our tea at three.
Spicy cookies
and an orange
just for you and me.

If you'll be my valentine
I'll make you funny faces.
You can make them
back at me
when we go different places.

If you'll be my valentine
then I'll be one for you.
We'll love the trees
and all the world . . .

We'll love each other, too.

Happy Valentine's Day.